Joseph Beldam

The Origin and Use of the Royston Cave

being the substance of a sketch some time since presented to the Royal

Society of Antiquaries by the late Joseph Beldam

Joseph Beldam

The Origin and Use of the Royston Cave
*being the substance of a sketch some time since presented to the Royal Society of
Antiquaries by the late Joseph Beldam*

ISBN/EAN: 9783337426705

Printed in Europe, USA, Canada, Australia, Japan

Cover: Foto ©Andreas Hilbeck / pixelio.de

More available books at **www.hansebooks.com**

THE ORIGIN AND USE

OF

THE ROYSTON CAVE

BEING

THE SUBSTANCE OF A REPORT,

SOME TIME SINCE PRESENTED TO

THE ROYAL SOCIETY OF ANTIQUARIES.

BY THE LATE

JOSEPH BELDAM, ESQ.

F. S. A., F. R. G. S.,

MEMBER OF THE ARCHÆOLOGICAL INSTITUTE OF GREAT BRITAIN
AND IRELAND.

Third Edition.

ROYSTON :

PUBLISHED BY JOHN WARREN.

M.DCCC.LXXXIV.

PREFACE TO THE THIRD EDITION.

THE increased value now universally accorded to antiquarian researches has suggested to me the desirability of issuing in a more portable form the "HISTORY OF ROYSTON CAVE," written by my late Uncle, JOSEPH BELDAM, ESQ., for the Antiquarian Society of London. Apart from its local interest, this Cave, which is unique of its kind, has attained an important celebrity beyond the County.

VALENTINE E. BELDAM.

BANYERS, ROYSTON,
October, 1884.

THE ROYSTON CAVE.

INTRODUCTION.

MORE than a century has elapsed since a fortunate accident led to the discovery of one of the most interesting specimens of antiquity possessed by this or any other country—the ROYSTON CAVE. So great was the curiosity occasioned by this singular occurrence, that it immediately gave rise to a warm controversy between two eminent archæologists of the day, Dr. William Stukeley and the Rev. Charles Parkin, in the course of which, though both parties displayed abundant learning and ingenuity, the cause of truth suffered much from their mutual loss of temper, and the too eager desire on both sides to establish a rival theory. The foibles of these literary combatants have passed away. And the present age, distinguished, unquestionably, by a much higher sense of the national value of the archæological studies, when rightly conducted, and aided likewise by a more enlarged experience of archæological probabilities, seems to be in a better position to exercise an impartial and correct judgment on the points disputed. Recent researches also have contributed, in some degree, to throw additional light on the origin and use of this remarkable excavation. The result has been a revival of curiosity in several quarters, which has ended in a request, now complied with, to publish the substance of a Report, presented a few years ago to the Royal Society of

Antiquaries. In respect to which paper it need only be stated, that the desire to make the subject strictly popular, has led to the omission of numerous quotations and references, which would have encumbered the page, without adding in equal proportion to the gratification of the general reader.

THE TOWN OF ROYSTON AND ITS VICINITY.

Our present object being merely a history of the Cave, any further description of the town and neighbourhood than may be necessary to decide upon the origin and use of this remarkable excavation must be deemed superfluous.

A very brief notice of the locality will suffice for this purpose. The town of Royston stands partly in Cambridge-shire and partly in Hertfordshire, on a range of chalk downs which extend through the kingdom from east to west, and precisely at the point of junction of two military roads of great antiquity, which here cross each other ; one called the Ermen Street, commencing, as it is supposed, on the coast of Sussex, and proceeding through Stamford and Lincoln, into the northern counties ; the other called the Ikenhilde Street, probably commencing in Dorsetshire, and following the chalk downs eastward through Dunstable and Ickleton, to Ickleham in Suffolk.

Near Royston two vicinal roads ran parallel to the Ikenhilde Street, one along the brow of the hills, and still called in some parts, the Ridgeway ; the other skirting the northern edge of the downs, and still known by the name of the Ashwell Way.

The whole country abounds with British, Roman, and Saxon antiquities. Along the ancient ways, especially in the direction of the Ikenhilde Street, are numerous Roman military posts, cemeteries and sepulchral remains, including the Roman Villa and Cemetery at Litlington ; and Roman coins of most of the imperial reigns are frequently found. Dr. Stukeley and the Rev. Charles Parkin, both take it for granted that a Roman town or Station existed on the site of the present town ; founding their opinion on the well-known Roman custom of erecting a station at the junction of their principal roads. It must be confessed, however, that this reasoning is not quite conclusive ; and no certain vestiges of Roman habitations can be affirmed to have been ever discovered. But the absence of these may, perhaps, be sufficiently accounted for, in so exposed a country, by the subsequent ravages of Pictish, Saxon, and Danish invaders, each bent on the destruction of the works of their pre-decessors. And some confirmation is given to the idea of a Roman station, by the recent discovery of several ancient shafts or pits similar to those found at Chesterford, and other confessedly Roman sites.

Proofs of a successive British and Saxon occupation, however, are everywhere seen. It cannot be doubted, that on the beautiful turf around, each of these ancient races in turn pastured their flocks, celebrated their games, marshalled their forces, and for very many ages in succession buried their illustrious dead. Their funereal mounds still form the most picturesque feature of the landscape, and, as we shall presently have occasion to observe, may possibly be able to contest with Lady Rosia herself the honour of giving their name to the modern town.

But whatever may have been the antecedent history of the spot, we learn from the celebrated Camden, that at the time of the Norman Conquest no town existed here. The place was not even mentioned by name in Domesday Book. From this, however, we are by no means obliged to conclude that it was an absolute solitude. We must bear in mind, that having at that time no parochial existence, it could not be noticed in the Norman record of parishes ; and all that could be then said was contained in the recitals of the various fees and lordships which extended over it. Something like proof, moreover, that the spot was in fact inhabited by a British tribe, may be gathered, not only from the innumerable British tumuli in the vicinity, but from the discovery of various circular floors and cuttings in the chalk, usually considered to mark the sites of ancient British dwellings ; and evidences of a Saxon population may be equally inferred from the disclosure of numerous Saxon graves, both around and within the limits of the town ; as well as from the continued usage of a Saxon appellation to a part of it (the Fleet or *Flett* end), which seems clearly to indicate one or more habitations on the spot at a period anterior to the Norman survey, not specifically noticed, but included, of course, in the general recitals of Bassingbourne parish, to which they belong.

THE OLD CROSS.

At the junction of these two ancient military roads formerly stood the old cross ; and as we shall probably be able to establish a connexion between the Cave and the Cross, it will not be altogether beside our purpose to offer a few remarks upon the latter. The exact position of this venerable monument is not known, but it may be presumed to have stood in the south-east angle of the roads, somewhere between the dome of the Cave and the line of the Ermen Street, being in the parish of Barkway, and in the fee of the Lordship of Newsells. It may have occupied the site of an earlier monument, and possibly even in Roman times. It was certainly the practice of that people to set up a Hermes at crossways for the guidance and protection of travellers; and it was not less common among the Saxons to erect a cross for similar purposes; but the previous existence of a monument in this place cannot be carried beyond conjecture. Unfortunately for the question, also, of its Saxon or Norman origin, the form of the historical Cross cannot now be determined, the upper part having been long since destroyed. But the foot-stone, which still exists, is properly described by Stukeley, as "a flattish "stone of very great bulk, with a square hole, or mortaise, "in the centre, wherein was let the foot of the upright stone, "or tenon, which was properly the cross." And this interesting relic, after several migrations,—first to the opposite corner of the street, where it was seen by Stukeley, and next to the Market Hill, has lately been removed to the garden of the Royston Institute.

Camden, who is a great authority on most questions, but who seems in the present instance to have contented himself with local tradition, ascribes the erection of this Cross to "a famous Lady Rosia, by some supposed," he says, "to have been Countess of Norfolk, about the time of "the Norman Conquest, which Cross," he adds, "was called "after her name, Royse's Cross, till Eustace de Marc founded, "just by it, a Priory, dedicated to St. Thomas à Becket, the "Martyr of Canterbury; upon which occasion inns came to "be built, and by degrees it became a town, which instead "of Royse's Cross, took the name of Royse's Town, after- "wards contracted to Royston."

An inspection of the earliest deeds connected with this Priory will shew that Camden 'was not quite accurate on that subject; and he may have been misled as to the origin of the Cross. A great probability undoubtedly exists, that the earliest proprietors of the fee of Newsells had something to do, either with its erection or its restoration ; a probability helped by the fact, that among the members and nearest connexions of that noble family, shortly after the Conquest, there actually were several ladies who bore the name of " Rosia." But Camden's statement by no means identifies the lady to whom the Cross, even in this case, should be ascribed. And, allowing some ground for the tradition, we should be disposed to refer it to the elder Lady Rosia, the wife of Eudo Dapifer, the first Norman possessor of the fee, and the grandmother, by marriage, of Dr. Stukeley's heroine, rather than to the second Lady Rosia, whom he so gratuitously prefers.

There are other writers, however, who, judging as well from the old Roman and Saxon practice above mentioned, as from the internal testimony of the Priory deeds, and the probable etymology of ancient words, have been disposed to attribute a much earlier date to this Cross. Among these, the Rev. Mr. Parkins argues, with some force, that the style and title of the Priory, founded in the lifetime of the second Lady Rosia, and called after the name of the Cross, " *De Cruce Roœsie*," certainly imply that the Cross itself was at that time of considerable fame, and probably of considerable antiquity. And this inference seems strengthened by the local and vernacular name of the spot, frequently occurring in the earliest Priory deeds, and latinized into " *Roœsie*," which is variously spelt " *Roys*," " *Roes*," " *Rous*," and " *Roheys*," words which certainly have much of a Scandinavian character, and are not so easily derived from a female Christian name.

Salmon, the antiquary of the county, adopting a similar view, cites the learned Dane, Olaus Wormius, to prove, that among the northern nations, the practice of burning the dead, and heaping a mound over their ashes, was known by the name of "*Roiser*," and the tumulus itself, by the name of "*Roise*." And various Saxon words, almost identical in sound, and of similar import, such as "*Hreaws*," pronounced "*Raws*," meaning a funeral; "*Reowes*," pronounced "*Roes*," signifying sorrow or mourning; and "*Rowes*," or "*Rous*," implying rest or repose, all appear to confirm the Scandinavian origin of the name, and raise a strong presumption that the original cross was so called, either from some remarkable funereal mound erected on the spot, or from those numerous tumuli in the neighbourhood, which in its originally wild and open condition, must have formed the chief characteristic of the country, and would naturally suggest the appellation.

Stukeley himself, while strenuously maintaining the claims of the Lady Rosia to the honour of erecting the Royston Cross, fully admits that the practice was very common in Saxon times for religious persons to build such monuments by the wayside, and especially where several roads met. And he adds, that hermits' cells were often placed near them, where, in accordance with the superstition of the age, recluses spent their remaining days in directing travellers, and in praying for their safety and welfare.

The most reasonable conclusion, as we think, to be drawn from the whole, is, that an earlier cross did actually exist here, before the Norman Conquest; which having been subsequently rebuilt or repaired by one of the pious ladies of the manor of Newsells, in whose domain it stood, and whose Christian name was Rosia, the resemblance of this name to the former pagan name by which it was known, enabled the monks of a later age easily to substitute the one for the other, and thus to transfer the honour of the foundation to a member of the noble house to which they owed their own endowment.

DISCOVERY OF THE CAVE, AND ITS
FIRST APPEARANCE.

The Cave was discovered by accident, in the month of August, 1742, and was almost immediately afterwards visited by the Rev. George North, of Caldecot, a member of the Society of Antiquaries, at their special request. Its position has been already indicated as being in the south-east angle of the two main roads, and nearly below the Cross. In a letter, addressed to the learned Society in the following month of September, Mr. North states, that on examination, he had found the Cave, not only different from what he had apprehended, but from anything he ever saw before.' The workmen, however, had not then reached the bottom by 8 feet, for which reason he could give but an imperfect account of it. But by way of illustration, he enclosed a rough drawing of its appearance at that stage, a copy of which will be seen among the sketches now presented to the reader. Mr. North, after giving a brief description of the place and the circumstances of the discovery, to which we shall presently advert, expressed his conviction that the whole was the work of remote ages, and certainly anterior to the existence of a town on the spot. He stated, however, that no relics had as yet been found, except a human skull and a few decayed bones, fragments of a small drinking cup of common brown earth, marked with yellow spots, and a piece of brass without any figure or inscription on it. He added that there was no tradition in the town to lead to the design of the excavation.

Dr. Stukeley, the celebrated secretary, to the Society, shortly afterwards went down, and found the place entirely cleared. He repeated his visit somewhat later, and made sketches of the interior, which he published with an account of the discovery. But he records the finding of no additional relics, except a small seal of pipe-clay, marked with a fleur-de-lys, which afterwards came into his possession.

From the respective statements of these two antiquaries, we learn, that in the year above mentioned, the town's people had occasion to set down a post in the Mercat House, which then stood above it, and was used as a cheese and butter market by the mercat women. In digging beneath the bench on which these women were accustomed to sit, the workmen struck upon a mill-stone laid underground, at the depth of about a foot, having a hole in the centre. Finding that there was a cavity beneath, they tried its depth by a plumb line, which descended 16 feet. This induced them to remove the stone, which covered a shaft of about 2 feet in diameter, with foot-holes cut into the sides, at equal distances, and opposite each other, like the steps of a ladder. This shaft, we are informed, was quite circular and perpendicular. A boy was first let down into it, and afterwards a slender man, with a lighted candle, who ascertained that it passed through an opening about 4 feet in height into another cavity, which was filled with loose earth, yet not touching the wall, which he saw to the right and left. The people now entertained a notion of great treasure hid in this place, and some workmen enlarged the descent.   Then, with buckets and a well-kirb, they set to work in earnest to draw up the earth and rubbish. The vast concourse of people now becoming very troublesome, they were obliged to work by night, till, at length, by unwearied diligence, after raising two hundred loads of earth, they quite exhausted it.

And "then fully appeared," writes Dr. Stukeley, with

the genuine enthusiasm of an antiquary, "this agreeable
"subterranean recess, hewn out of pure chalk. 'Tis of an
"elegant bell-like, or rather mitral form, well turned, and
"exactly circular,"—an observation, however, which is not
quite correct.   "The effect," he goes on to say, "is very
"pleasing.   The light of the candles scarce reaches the top,
"and that gloominess overhead increases the solemnity of
"the place.   All around the sides, it is adorned with
"imagery, in basso relievo, of crucifixes, saints, martyrs,
"and historical pieces.   They are cut with a design and
"rudeness suitable to the time, which was soon after the
"Conquest.   A kind of broad bench goes quite round the
"floor next the wall, broader than a step, and not quite
"so high as a seat.   This bench is cut off in the eastern
"point by the grave, which is dug deeper into the chalk."

The actual appearance of the Cave, at this period,
being of some consequence to our further enquiries, a few
more particulars will be added, respecting the dome, which
does not seem, however, to have undergone any close
examination.   Dr. Stukeley, who saw it only from the
bottom, and by candle-light, merely adverts to a piece of
masonry visible near the top, which they who viewed it
near, he says, told him, was made of brick, tile, and stone,
laid in good mortar, and thought it might have been done
to mend a defective part in the chalk, while Stukeley
himself conjectured that it might be the original descent,
afterwards walled up when the second shaft was made.
Mr. North, who made his observations before the cave was
emptied, and therefore from a higher level, remarks that a
portion of the dome had been either repaired or strengthened
with free-stone and tiles, placed edgeways ; and that almost
opposite the shaft through which he entered, there appeared the top of an arch, which the workmen imagined

might lead to the ancient way into it, concluding from the narrowness of this shaft that it was designed only for a vent or air-hole. He also remarks, that the top or crown-work of the dome was curiously composed of tile work, and within a foot of the street above ; and further, that some persons thought a passage ran from the Cave to the Priory, a notion which was discredited, however, by Stukeley.

The subsequent discovery of a date in this part of the Cave gives rise to regret that a more careful inspection and a fuller report had not been made by the two first visitors. All that we can now gather from their statements is, that no inscription was then perceived ; that the masonry concealing the supposed passage was at that time entire ; and that the dome had not then been opened to the surface. Before we pass on to another division of our subject, it may be right to perpetuate the fact recorded by Stukeley, that Mr. George Lettis, probably the bailiff of the manor, and William Lilley, a tailor and salesman, who lived in the adjoining house, where the chief movers in opening and clearing the place.

SUBSEQUENT ALTERATIONS AND PRESENT APPEARANCE.

Before we proceed to more recent investigations, it will be proper to state that, since the time of Stukeley and North, several changes have occurred, considerably altering the appearance of the place.

In their day, it will be borne in mind, the entrance was by a narrow shaft in the northern side of the Cave. The crown of the dome had not then been pierced, and the place could only be seen by artificial lights. The masonry concealing the opening of the shaft on the eastern side had

not been disturbed.   And the part which Stukeley called
the grave, had not been made up to the level of the podium
or broad step which encircles the floor.

The present entrance is by an arch opening into the
bottom of the Cave, just above the grave, and on the
eastern side ;   and is reached by means of a gradually
descending passage, 72 feet in length, passing under the
Ikenhilde Street, which was cut through the solid chalk,
in the year 1790, by Thomas Watson, a bricklayer, who
occupied the Town House, on the opposite side, and who
employed his workmen during a hard winter in accom-
plishing this difficult task.   A glimmering light is now also
admitted through a grated opening in the dome, which was
probably made at the same time.   And, either then, or at
some other time unknown, the masonry closing the arch on
the eastern side of the doom was broken down, plainly
exposing another shaft, which now appears above.

The design of affording greater facilities for the inspection of the Cave, was, by these means, accomplished ; and
the labour and expense of the projector, were, in the sequel,
amply repaid.   Among the numerous distinguished
personages who have since visited it, may be mentioned
the late King of the French, Louis XVIII., induced,
possibly, by Stukeley's description of the historical figures,
to pay this homage to the memory of his ancestor, Louis
VII.   And many individuals are still living, who remember
the patriotic zeal and comical effect with which the old
Widow Watson, as pythoness of the Cave, was accustomed
to descant on the exploits and piety of its heroes and
heroines, mixing up the legends of saints with the fables of
Stukeley, and confidently supporting her statements, by
quotations from history, which she humorously called
the " Book of Kings."

LATER EXAMINATION AND FURTHER DESCRIPTION.

In the year 1852, a fresh and more careful examination of the Cave was made by Mr. Beldam, assisted by his friend, Mr. Edmund Nunn, the honorary curator of the Royston Museum : and from a manuscript report, afterwards presented to the Antiquarian Society, we select the following particulars.

The height of the Cave from the floor to the top of the dome, is about 25½ feet ; the length of the aperture leading up to the surface is about 2 feet ; making together, with the thickness of the crownwork at the top of the dome, about 28 feet. The bottom is not quite circular : the widest diameter being from east to west. The diameter from north to south is about 17 feet, and from east to west about 17 feet 6 inches, the difference being occasioned by the groove of the eastern shaft, which descends this side, and has not been accurately worked into the circle.

The broad step, or podium, which surrounds the floor, is octagonal, and is about 8 inches in height, by 3 feet in width, being now carried over the part which Stukeley calls the grave ; upon which is now likewise placed an ancient millstone, probably the same that closed the shaft discovered in 1742.

About 8 feet above the floor a cornice runs round the walls, cut in a reticulated or diamond pattern, about 2 feet in breadth, and receding, as it rises, about 6 inches ; making the diameter of the lower part of the dome, which springs from it, about 18 feet. The cornice is not, however, continued over the grave, but descends with a curve on one side, leaving the space above it unornamented and in its original rude condition. Almost the whole circle between the

B

podium and the cornice has been sculptured in low relief,
as described by Stukeley, with crucifixes, saints, martyrs,
and historical pieces ; and many of these, if not all, have
been coloured.   Vestiges of red, blue, and yellow, are
visible in various places ; and the relief of the figures
has been assisted by a darker pigment.   Above the cornice,
rude figures and heraldic devices are also here and there cut
or scratched into the chalk, but none in relief.   In different
parts of the Cave, both above and below the cornice, deep
cavities, or recesses, of various forms and sizes, some of
them oblong and others oven-shaped, are irregularly cut
into the wall, closely resembling olla-holes, niches, and
recesses, usually seen in Roman, Etruscan, and Phenician
tombs.   One of these cavities above the cornice is about
4 feet 6 inches in length, by about 2 feet 6 inches in
height ; and another in a similar position, about 2 feet
6 inches in length, with a corresponding height.   Besides
which, innumerable small crosses, perforations, and un-
intelligible devices are discernible in all directions.

Immediately above the grave, at the height of about
17 feet appears the masonry, supposed by Stukeley and
North to have concealed the original entrance.   The two
lower courses only of this masonry now remain, formed
of blocks of chalk neatly chiseled, and coloured red,
giving them the appearance of brickwork.   The shaft is
seen above them, here impinging on the dome, and still
partially filled with earth, which, on examination, was found
to be mixed with small fragments of the bones of animals,
and a few pieces of mediæval pottery, but no human bones.
The perpendicular course of the shaft, proved that it formed
no portion of a passage leading to the Priory.

The inspection of this part of the Cave was accomplished
by means of ladders and torch-light ; and led to the

discovery of certain numerical figures carefully and artistically cut into the end block of the upper course, giving the date of " 1347," which, if genuine as their appearance certainly indicates, may assist in tracing the transition through which Arabic numerals have passed in this country ; and furnish evidence of the continued use of the crypt. Below this masonry, the shaft evidently expanded as it descended to the grave ; and the chalk in this part of the Cave never having been dressed to correspond with the surrounding surface, exhibits, as already stated, the marks of an extreme and primeval antiquity.

THE GRAVE.

The grave being opened, was found to range exactly with the shouldering of the shaft above.   Its length proved to be about 7 feet 6 inches ; its depth below the floor about 2 feet ; and its width about 3 feet. To a certain depth it had been evidently disturbed, but the bottom had never been moved. It was found to contain a variety of objects, which, had they been seen by Stukeley, must have sadly disconcerted his theory of the origin and use of the place. Among these may be mentioned, *first*, as being nearest the surface, fragments of red bricks, described by him, as enclosing the grave, not improbably Norman or Early English ; and others somewhat more Roman in their character. Marks of cremation appeared on several of these as well as in other parts of the grave. *Secondly*, fragments of oak of great thickness, studded with large clout-headed nails, and pieces of iron, apparently, the mountings of a small oblong chest. *Thirdly*, a rude iron instrument, probably used for holding a light, and various pieces of iron much corroded. *Fourthly*, a large lump of charcoal, powdered with sulphur. *Fifthly*, intermixed with the above, a large quantity of the bones of animals ; but none of them human. Specimens of these being submitted to Professors Owen and Quekett, were pronounced to be of the kind usually found in bone shafts and British graves; such, for instance, as bones of the ox, the hog, the hare, and the goat or sheep. In the lowest stratum, which required the pick-axe to move it, were found the bones of a young deer ; and the vertebræ of a small fish. There were, moreover, many spherical stones, of the class called "aëtite," or "eagle stone," known also to the ancients as the "lapis pregnans," and believed by them to be endowed with medicinal and magical properties ; and, finally, fragments of glass, of leather, of wood, and some other articles of doubtful character.

ORIGINAL CONSTRUCTION AND PURPOSE OF THE CAVE.

An attentive consideration of the articles found in the grave, even supposing a few of them to have been subsequently introduced, fully verified the presumption raised by the peculiarly crippled and time-worn aspect of the wall above, that the so-called grave was nothing more than a continuation below the floor, of the ancient eastern shaft ; and it consequently furnished a probable clue to the subsequent formation and original design of the whole. It seemed clear, that this shaft, in connexion with that on the northern side of the Cave, discovered in 1742, and of which the traces downward are visible as low as the floor, was the original excavation, and that from one or both of these, by the same, or by successive operations, one or more primitive chambers were horizontally opened, which at length assumed the form of the present Cave. It might be reasonably inferred, that this process began from the eastern shaft, with the upper part of the dome, and, judging from the large and deep niches cut in this part, it might be also presumed that the floor of the first excavation was but a little below them. The lower half of the Cave, on this supposition, with its numerous niches and recesses, was sunk at a later period. A method similar to this may be observed in the shafts and sepulchral chambers recently discovered at Stone.

The subject, however, of ancient shafts and subterranean chambers deserves a little further consideration.

The formation of shafts seems common to all ages and countries. They were opened for mining, for sanitary, for ceremonial, and for sepulchral purposes. Man seems to have been always a burrowing animal. But their most common use was, probably, always sepulchral ; either for the purpose of actual interment, or as a means of access to chambers intended for that object. Thus the Egyptians often buried their dead in shafts. The tombs of the Scythians, as recent discoveries in the Crimea have shown and likewise those of the old Etruscans, were commonly approached by means of shafts. The interment of the poor at Rome in shafts or wells, called "puticoli," gave an historical celebrity to the Esquiline Hill. And even when not designed to contain the ashes of the dead, they seem to have been frequently employed to deposit the embers of the funereal fire, the bones of the funereal feast, the pottery used and broken on these and other sacred occasions ; and some-times, also for the ornaments and relics of the departed.

Allusion has been already made to the existence of ancient shafts at Royston ; and many others have been discovered in different parts of the kingdom. Among them may be specially mentioned those at Ewell in Surrey, at Boxmoor in Hertfordshire, at Stone in Buckinghamshire, at

Chadwell in Essex, at Crayford in Kent, and numbers
more recently opened by the present Lord Braybrooke at
Chesterford. The contents of most of them seem clearly
to prove a Romano-British origin, and a sepulchral or
religious purpose. But the indications at Royston are not
so decisive, though of a similar kind. The objects found in
the shaft at the Cave create some uncertainty also, as to
its original design, and make it doubtful whether its first
purpose was a place of deposit or a means of access only
to the chamber beyond; for if the latter, we must conclude
that it was afterwards accommodated to the ulterior
purpose of the Cave. What that purpose was has yet to be
considered.

Excavated chambers of this kind appear to have been
as common and as various in their use as the ancient shafts.
They were adapted to the habits, customs, and necessities of
the different countries where they are found. In our own
country, and among its earliest inhabitants, we learn from
the ancient historians that they were most commonly used,
either as places of refuge and concealment, or for the
deposit of grain and other stores; but it was not the
ordinary practice of the Celts and Scandinavians to bury in
them. Any sepulchral application, therefore, must be
presumed to have occurred in a Romano-British period. In
most other countries, however, their principal object appears
to have been always sepulchral; and they were so used,
either with or without the accompaniment of the shaft.
Both kinds abound in Egypt, in Palestine, in the Crimea, in
Etruria, and in most other parts of the Roman Empire.

Hence the original purpose of the Royston Cave, if of
purely British origin, could scarcely have been sepulchral.
It bears, indeed, a strong resemblance, in form and dimen-
sion, to the ancient British habitation; and certain marks

and decorations in its oldest parts, such as indentations and punctures, giving a diapered appearance to the surface, are very similar to what is seen in confessedly Druidical and Phenician structures. But this by no means militates against the probability of its subsequent appropriation to the use of a Roman sepulchre.

The Roman underground sepulchres, it is true, were not generally of a conical form, but nothing was more common with them than to appropriate the designs and devices of a conquered people. Mr. Akerman, the present learned Secretary of the Antiquarian Society, in a recent paper in *Archæologia*, vol. xxxiv., p. 27, on the Roman remains at Stone, and which contains references to most of the other shafts to be met with in this country, expresses a firm conviction that the Royston Cave was at one time a Roman sepulchre. He quotes also an instance of a similar sepulchre, discovered many years since on the Aventine hill at Rome; the only difference of form in that case being, that the shaft entered at the top of the dome, instead of at the side. Few persons, indeed, who have a fresh recollection of the old Tombs of Italy, with their niches and recesses for urns, and cists and lamps, and votive offerings—their ornamented cornices, and benches for the repose of the dead —will fail to discover in the Royston Cave marks of similar design and similar uses. Nor will the disappearance of the many funereal objects it may once have contained in any considerable degree lessen the probability, after so long a dedication to the purposes of Christian worship.

COMPARISON WITH ORIENTAL CAVES.

Admitting this general resemblance, however, it must still be confessed, that among the ancient sepulchres of Europe, there are none which correspond exactly with the

Royston Cave ; and whether its present form existed in
Roman times, or is the result of more recent modifications,
we are led to conclude that its precise model was, most
probably, derived from the East ; a conclusion which need
not at all disturb our belief in its early Roman occupation.

It is certain that ancient caves do exist in Palestine,
which, in form and circumstance, and to some extent also in
decoration, approximate so nearly to the Royston Cave,
that if any historical connexion could be established
between them, it would scarcely seem doubtful that the
one is a copy of the other. Such a connexion we shall now
endeavour to show, possibly even in Roman times, but more
certainly at a later period.

The caves in question are fully described by Professor
Robinson, of America, in his *Biblical Researches*, vol. ii.,
p. 353 et seq. He there states, that in the vicinity of Deir
Dubban, at no great distance from Gaza and Askelon, where
the soil scarcely covers the chalky rock, he visited certain
caves, excavated into the form of tall domes or bell-shaped
apartments, ranging in height from 20 to 30 feet ; and in
diameter from 10 or 12 to 20 or 30 feet or more. The top of
these domes usually terminates in a small circular opening
for the admission of light and air. These dome-shaped
caverns, he adds, are mostly in clusters, three or four
together. They are all hewn regularly. Some of them are
ornamented, either near the bottom or high up, or both,
with rows of small holds or niches, like pigeon holes,
extending quite round. And in one of the caves he observed
crosses cut into the walls. In like manner, at Beit Jibrin,
he saw numerous caves of a similar form, cut into the same
chalky soil. In one cave he also remarked a line of
ornamental work about 10 feet above the floor, resembling
a sort of cornice ; and the whole hill appeared to have been

perforated with caves of a similar kind. They seemed, he says, to be innumerable in that neighbourhood. It must be borne in mind, that Dr. Robinson, in describing these caves, could scarcely have known of the existence of that at Royston. He does not pretend to decide on their age or use. His acquaintance with such subjects appears, indeed, from other parts of his work, to have been limited ; but he suggests that they may have been inhabited by a colony of Edomites, from the resemblance they bear to some excavations at Petra. It is, at least, certain that the descendants of Esau did occupy this district several centuries before the Christian æra ; and Herod the Great was born at Askelon.

But any historical connexion with the Royston Cave must be sought for at a later period. It may possibly be found in the circumstance that these caves were in the vicinity of the ancient city of Eleutheropolis, and that after the Roman conquest they were almost certainly used as columbaria or cemeteries by the inhabitants. This city is known to have been one of those most highly favoured by the Emperor Severus, during his successful administration of the East. The Empress Julia was also a native of that part of the empire. Assuming, then, that the form of the Royston Cave has undergone no change since Roman times, it does not seem wholly improbable, that, as this emperor spent so much of his after life in Britain, the Royston Cave may owe its existence to the officers of some veteran legion, who may have accompanied him to this country, and may have been quartered at one of the military posts in this neighbourhood. At any rate, numerous coins of this emperor and his family, as well as moulds for coining, found in this vicinity, show how closely the country was occupied by the Romans at that period.

If, on the other hand, we conclude that the form of the Royston Cave has undergone some change since those imperial times, we shall be able to find other and still stronger probabilities of its connexion with the Oriental caves at a later period. Perhaps no stronger argument can be advanced, than the fact that the district in which these caves abound, was one of the great battle fields of the early Crusaders. It was here that they built their famous fortresses of El Hasi and Blanche Garde ; and the country all around was the scene of the adventures and triumphs of Richard Cœur de Lion, and his puissant chivalry. Again, whatever may have been the former purpose of these caves they must, at a period subsequent to the Christain æra,— when Palestine swarmed with anchorites,—have become, in all probability, like most other grottos and tombs in that country,—the abode of hermits and recluses ; and, as such, must have been known and respected by the Christian leaders. It seems most natural, therefore, to trace this singular correspondence of form to the piety of some distinguished Crusader, anxious on his return to his own country to perpetuate the memory of former exploits, and to exhibit his devotion in a manner most accordant with the ideas and superstitions of his age.

CONVERSION INTO A CHRISTIAN ORATORY.

However we may decide on these points, it is certain that a time did arrive when the Cave became appropriated to Christian worship ; and it is to the period of the early Crusades that this change may be most reasonably referred. In that age, the attention of all Europe was directed towards the East. Everything was deemed sacred which came from that region. The ecclesiastical structures and practices of the day, borrowed largely from eastern models ; and no greater act of piety could then be imagined than the founding and endowing oratories and hermitages, resembling those which had been devoutly visited and venerated in the Holy Land.

Now, among the Christian knights who fought most gallantly on the plains of Askelon and Gaza, were some of the descendants and near connections of Eudo Dapifer, Lord of the Manor of Newsells.

With this period, also, most nearly agrees the style of its principal decorations. And the greater part of its sculptures, so far as we can understand them, appears to belong to the same age.

Connecting these circumstances together, a strong presumption appears to be raised, that the ultimate design and ornamentation are due to some noble member of the early Newsells family ; and though we are obliged to reject Dr. Stukeley's visionary notion of Lady Rosia's personal share in this business, there is some reason to believe that the work may be mainly ascribed to the devotion and liberality of one of her sons, probably William de Magnaville, her favourite son, a companion in the exploits of King Richard, and one of his most gallant comrades in the wars of Palestine. But the story of Lady Rosia's subsequent retirement to this oratory, and of the execution of the sculpture with her own hand, is purely imaginary ; and the fiction of her interment in this place is contradicted by the best historical evidence.

DECORATIONS OF THE ORATORY.

It has already been stated that the entire space between the cornice and the floor, with the exception of the part down which the eastern shaft descends, has been decorated with sculptures, representing crucifixes, saints, martyrs, and historical personages. These do not seem to have been all executed by the same person, nor, probably, at precisely the same time; but all of them, notwithstanding their rude and inartificial manner, produce a striking effect. And most, if not all of them, have been coloured, though perhaps at a later period. The only sculptures in this country that can be compared to them, are certain effigies carved into the chalk walls of the castle at Guildford, in Surrey, which are likely to have been of the same period.

Before we proceed to describe the principal groups, we shall offer a few preliminary remarks on their probable age, under the head of Costumes, Armour, Architectural Designs, and Heraldic Devices.

1. On the subject of costumes, particularly the head-dresses of the ladies, Stukeley and Parkin disagree, the former assigning them, as we think correctly, to the twelfth century, the latter to the fourteenth or fifteenth. It must be admitted, that similar costumes prevailed at both periods, and the question must, therefore, be rather decided by the probable import of the stories to which they belong. In like manner, the helmets in general, and the coiffures of the men afford no certain criterion; though several of them are certainly of a crusading age. The crowns, coronets, and mitres of Royal personages and prelates, are of a very antique form; but they may have been somewhat modified by the fancy of the artist.

2. The Armour in general seems antecedent to the period when the whole person was cased in steel; and, together with the absence of beards, appears to indicate the fashion of the twelfth or thirteenth century.

3. The Architectural Designs, which are few, are of the Norman and Early English character.

4. The Heraldic Devices, in the opinion of competent judges, of the Herald's College, to whom they have been submitted, belong to an age anterior to the general use of family badges, and may consequently be assigned to the eleventh or twelfth century. The kite-shaped and small circular shields can hardly belong to a later period.

Before we quit this head, we must, however, advert to a particular shield, which became the subject of hot dispute between Stukeley and Parkin ; the former claiming it for a Beauchamp, the father of Lady Rosia's second husband, the latter, for a much later member of the same family. The old story of the battle of the shield was here revived ; but in this case, instead of both knights being in the right, both were in the wrong, both evidently mistaking the device about which they quarrelled. There is, perhaps, more excuse for Parkin, who, for aught we can gather, never entered the Cave. The fact, however, is, that the six cross crosslets in dispute, appear to be simply two letters, "H.K.," above the fess, with a Calvary cross beneath it.

The general result of this preliminary survey—admitting the possible existence of some later interpolations—appear strongly to favour the conclusion above stated, that the principal sculptures are of the age of Henry II. and Richard I.

EXPLANATION OF THE SCULPTURES.

The various groups and figures we are now about to describe, are irregularly distributed ; they are of different sizes ; refer to different subjects ; are probably the production of different artists ; and exhibit little unity of design. They harmonize chiefly by their general air of antiquity, and the quaintness which belongs to the efforts of a rude and superstitious age.

Several shrines adorn this oratory. The high altar, contrary to the usual practice, is on the western side. The shrine, and the legend of Saint Katharine, who appears to have been the patron saint of the place, are on the right and left of the high altar. The shrine of St. John Baptist and St. Thomas à Beckett (the patron saints of the Priory,) is on the southern side. The northern side exhibits the shrine and the legend of St. Christopher. The space between the effigy of St. Katharine and certain historical figures on the south-western side, is occupied by the effigies of St. Lawrence, St. Paul, the Holy Family, and the Flowering Cross. Various historical personages and scenes fill up the intervals ; and the eastern side is the only part which appears to have been left without decoration.

We shall consider these sculptures in the following order.

I.—THE HIGH ALTAR.

The oldest and most venerated object must, of course, have been the High Altar. It is represented by a square tablet sunk in the wall, on which is carved the scene of the crucifixion ;—our Saviour extended on the cross, the Virgin Mary on one side, and the beloved disciple on the other ; a heart and a hand is cut on either side ; the heart nearest the Virgin being composed of three lines, as indicative of most intense affection. The moulding of the tablet appears to have been removed at the bottom, to make room for the effigies of two royal persons, and a smaller crucifixion, which will be afterwards described. On the foot of the principal cross is cut a saltire or St. Andrew's cross.

The position of this altar, in the west, instead of the east of the oratory, has given rise to much speculation. Stukeley supposes it to have been placed here, in order to correspond, as nearly as possible, with the cross erected above ; thus enabling the worshipper to do homage to both at the same time. Another reason might be suggested by the necessity of leaving undisturbed the original entrance into the Cave, which was most probably by a ladder or steps descending from the eastern shaft ; and that portion of the Cave may, also, have been thought to be desecrated by its original pagan use.

II.—ST. CHRISTOPHER.

In describing the several groups, we will begin with those on the right hand of the modern entrance, which occupy the northern side of the Cave.

Immediately beyond the projecting shoulder of the eastern shaft, appears a group, consisting of two half-length personages above—one of them a female, the other a male clad in a toga or pallium ; a large figure is seen kneeling on one knee beneath them, as if in the act of receiving a burden ; and a small figure, almost effaced, is bestriding his neck. These figures have been painted red, and appear to represent Joseph and Mary placing the infant Saviour on the neck of St. Christopher, who is preparing to cross a river. The river is represented by the groove of the northern shaft, which descends here, and appears to have been scored to imitate running water.

On the other side of the river, St. Christopher appears again as a gigantic personage, in a short garment tucked up, and a huge staff in his hand still carrying the infant Saviour on his shoulder. This figure is almost identical in form with that cut into the chalk at Guildford Castle. At an early period, the effigy of St. Christopher was introduced into Christian churches. The legend was brought from the East by the Crusaders, and the saint having been a hermit, found an appropriate place in this oratory. He is represented to have been a Syrian or Canaanite, of enormous bulk, who, after his conversion, built himself a cell by the side of a river, and employed his great stature for the glory of God, in carrying pilgrims across. The superstition of the age assigned to him the special privilege of preventing tempests and earthquakes. His effigy was usually placed near the entrance of sacred buildings, as symbolical of baptismal admission to the Christian faith. There seems nothing unreasonable in supposing, with Stukeley, that these figures were cut about the year A.D. 1185, when there happened a terrible earthquake, such as was never known before in this country, followed by an eclipse of the sun, great thunderings, lightnings, and tempests, dreadful fires, and destruction of men and cattle. This saint being once on his travels, is reported to have struck his staff into the ground, which, in token of the truth of his doctrine, took root, and produced both flower and fruit.

We shall have occasion to remark a flowering staff, or cross, on the other side of the high altar, which Stukeley imagines, though perhaps incorrectly, has reference to this prodigy. Above the figure of St. Christopher is the entrance discovered by the town's people in 1742.

III.—LEGEND OF ST. KATHARINE THE MARTYR.

Next to St. Christopher is the legend of St. Katharine of Alexandria. It is related of this virgin and martyr, that being imprisoned by a cruel tyrant for twelve days without food, a dove was sent down by Providence to administer to her necessities. Her prison is here represented by a recess cut into the wall, and painted of a dark blue colour, which still remains. She first appears at the entrance, in a disconsolate position, and in a dress of yellowish hue. At the farther end of the prison, she again appears, lying on her back, her head placed on a pillow marked with a heart, and her whole person resting on a colossal arm and hand, painted in red, and engraved with a heart. It is presumed that these are symbols of her piety and dependence on Providence. Above the prison, appears the same out-stretched arm and hand, in the act of letting fly a dove, which hovers over the prisoner, with a wallet in its bill. The latter emblems are cut into the chalk, but not in relief, and have been likewise painted red. Below the prison are two deep oven-shaped cavities of unequal sizes ; one of them having a groove cut into the floor. They resemble other niches in different parts of the Cave, and were, probably, first designed for sepulchral deposits ; but in Christian times, they were appropriated to the service of the oratory, and were most likely used as piscinæ for the high altar, and as niches for lights, on St. Katharine's day, and other great festivals. Parkin has singularly mistaken the figure in prison for that of a man, and supposes the whole to represent the entombment of the Saviour, and Mary Magdalene waiting at the entrance.

Next in succession, comes the High Altar, already described.

IV.—EFFIGY OF ST. KATHARINE.

Immediately beyond the High Altar, appears the figure of St. Katharine in her beatified form, erect, holding the wheel, the instrument of her passion, in her right hand, and wearing a lofty crown, as being of the blood royal of Egypt. There is something singularly imaginative and spectral in this effigy. Occupying the place of honor in the oratory, we are led to conclude, that to this sainted lady, it was chiefly dedicated—a conclusion rather confirmed by the

existence of an ancient inn close by, still called the
"Katharine Wheel;" where we may presume that pilgrims
who came to honour her shrine were accustomed to resort,
and end their devotions in the usual orthodox manner.
Stukeley ascribes the preference shewn to St. Katharine in
this oratory, to a great victory obtained by the Crusaders
over Saladin and his hosts, on the plains of Ramleh, on
St. Katharine's day, 25th November, 1177; and as the
celebrated William de Magnaville, Lady Rosia's son, and
lord *in capite* of this manor, was present on that memorable
occasion, the conjecture seems by no means improbable.

V.—THE CROSS OF ST. HELENA.

Moving round in the same direction, the next object
probably represents the Cross of St. Helena, the mother of
Constantine the Great. Stukeley imagines it to be the staff
of St. Christopher, commonly called the Palmer's Staff.
But as the pretended discovery of the true cross by the first
Christian princess, must have been deemed an event of
greater consequence to the Romish church, than the private
adventures of any respectable saint; and as the singular
property ascribed by monkish writers to this cross, of
perpetually renewing itself, seems aptly symbolized by the
production of buds and flowers, we are disposed to conclude,
that the " Invention " of the cross is here represented.

VI.—THE HOLY FAMILY.

Beyond the cross, the figures divide into two lines. In
the upper line, nearest St. Katharine, appears the Holy
Family—Joseph, the Virgin, and the youthful Saviour. The
leading idea of pilgrimage, is here again portrayed; and
this group, most likely, represents the journey from
Jerusalem, after the feast of the Passover.

VII.—ST. LAURENCE.

In the same line to the left, is the effigy of St. Laurence with the instrument of passion in his hand. He wears a long garment, marked with a heart at the bottom. On his breast are cut two letters, I S, of somewhat doubtful antiquity. This saint suffered martyrdom in the reign of Gallienus, at Rome, and his death is celebrated on the 10th of August. The date is of considerable importance, as it will probably furnish the key to some of the historical portraits hereafter to be described.

VIII.—CONVERSION OF ST. PAUL.

Immediately below the Holy Family, in the second line, appears a horse overthrown and resting on its haunches,— a man unhelmed, and still holding by the bridle, but in the act of falling,—and a small circular shield, with a sword of extravagant length, flying from him. Stukeley naturally concludes this to mean the conversion of St. Paul, kept on the 25th of January ; and the length of the sword may be simply intended to remind the observer of the manner of his death. Parkin, however, rather absurdly as we think, discovers in this group the martyrdom of St. Hippolite, who was torn asunder by wild horses.

We can scarcely doubt, that the primary allusion here, was to St. Paul. But it may have been subsequently degraded into a satire on the family of William " Long Epée," or "Long Sword." This personage was allied by marriage to Lady Rosia, but opposed in politics to her family, and detested, both by priests and laity, for his inhumanity and sacrilege, in asserting the rights of King John. The clerical historians of the time, inform us, that the first Long Epée died an unnatural death : the second perished in Palestine : and the last of his race, being un-

horsed and indelibly disgraced at a great tournament, held
in the year 1250, died despised and young. It seems not
impossible, that the monks of the Priory, with a mixture, by
no means uncommon, with superstition and buffoonery, may
have contrived, by lengthening the sword, and somewhat
distorting the original figure, to make their devotion
subserve their revenge, in perpetuating the disgrace of a
fallen enemy.

IX.—WILLIAM THE LION, KING OF SCOTS.

In the same line with St. Paul, and immediately below
the effigy of St. Laurence, appears the half-length figure of
a royal personage, wearing an antique crown, and with
arms extended, in an attitude of surprise and alarm. On
the breast are cut the ancient initials, "WR"; and the
position, next to the falling saint, may not have been
without its meaning. This figure seems to form part of an
historical series, commencing on the southern side of the
Cave. We shall postpone our reasons for considering it the
portrait of William the Lion, until we reach it again from
the other side.

We now return to the entrance, and take the groups in
succession to the left.

The figures on this side of the Cave, are, for some
distance, nearly effaced. Not far from the entrance are two
deep recesses, probably, at first, intended for sepulchral
uses, but subsequently devoted to some purpose of the
Christian oratory. The first figure that can be traced, is
that of a person holding a ball, or globe, in his right hand ;
on the meaning of which we offer no conjecture.

X.—QUEEN ELEANOR.

The next is the half-length figure of a royal lady in a
cloister or cell, which forms part of an ecclesiastical edifice,

of Anglo-Norman or Early English architecture. The lady wears a crown, but has the air of being a prisoner; and probably represents Queen Eleanor, the wife of Henry II., who, in consequence of her intrigues and violence, was imprisoned by her husband for many years, and only liberated on the accession of her son, Richard I., Cœur de Lion. Parkin, however, supposes this figure to represent St. Katharine in prison. Our reason for differing from him will presently appear.

XI.—THE SHRINE OF ST. JOHN BAPTIST AND ST. THOMAS A BECKET.

Next to the royal prisoner, and only separated from her by a royal standard, and a figure, which probably represents the standard bearer, is the shrine of the two patron saints of the Priory Church, St. John Baptist and St. Thomas à Becket. Above the Shrine—which is a tablet sunk in the wall, and over the head of the Baptist, is a crucifix. St. John is represented as a venerable personage, bare-headed, and wearing a forked beard; of which this is the only instance in the Cave, except that of the Saviour, at the high altar. The figure is of three-quarters' length, the legs being merely scratched into the chalk, and possibly intended to appear as standing in the water. He wears a short tunic, and holds in his left hand, towards the figure of St. Thomas, a crown, surmounted by three drooping tendrils, probably indicating the palm and crown of martyrdom. St. Thomas is represented as a prelate of high degree, clothed in full canonicals, and wearing a lofty conical cap, or mitre. He holds in his right hand a globe, surmounted by a cross, and in his left a staff-crosier. An altar, marked with a cross, is cut into the space between these two saintly personages.

Stukeley supposes them to represent the Cardinal Octavian, as legate from the Pope, and Hugh de Nunant,

King Henry's chaplain, on a mission for the purpose of crowning his son John, King of Ireland. Another construction is, that the bearded man represents the Grand Master of the Hospitallers, bearing the royal standard and regalia of Jerusalem, attended by Heraclius the Patriarch; both these dignitaries having been deputed in the year 1185, to make a tender of the sovereignty of the Holy Land to Henry II., on condition of his hastening to its rescue from the Saracens. There seems some probability in this explanation. But on the whole we agree with Parkin, that it represents the Shrine of the two patron saints of the Priory; a confirmation of which is found in its historical connexion with the figures that follow, and likewise in the position of the cavity or niche beneath, which has certainly been used as a piscina.

XII.—KING HENRY II.

The formidable personage immediately beyond the shrine, is evidently the hero of the Cave. He is presumed to be Henry II., the reigning monarch of the time. He wears a low-crowned helmet; and a tabard girt about the waist, marked with a large cross on the breast, and a smaller one on either side. He holds a drawn sword in his right hand. Above him appears an array of troops; and further on are two other bodies of troops, headed by a prelate in a marshal vest, and wearing a peculiar kind of mitre; who seems to be offering an address, from behind a battlement or a pulpit. The person of the King, as well as those of St. John and of St. Thomas, has been painted red. Beneath them, a fish of singular form is scratched into the wall. And in the space between the king and the military bishop, on the other side, there are two cavities or niches, which were probably used as piscinæ to the shrines of the saints further on.

The whole of this series,—from the imprisoned Queen Eleanor, to the effigy of King William of Scotland, with the exception of certain genealogical figures near the military bishop, hereafter to be described,—appears to form a consecutive story, and to commemorate a remarkable event in the reign of King Henry, interesting alike to the clergy and the people of England, and peculiarly flattering to one of the patron saints of the Priory.

The circumstance was as follows :—

In the year A.D. 1175, great dissensions arose between King Henry and his sons, who were encouraged in their rebellion by their mother Queen Eleanor. The Queen in consequence, was placed in confinement, and continued a prisoner, as we have already stated, for most of the remainder of her husband's life. Henry's sons being supported by the kings of France and of Scotland, and by other powerful chieftains, King Henry prepared for war, and resolved to combat his enemies, both at home and abroad. While still lingering in Normandy, William the Lion of Scotland made an incursion into the northern counties, where he committed great ravages ; when Geoffrey, bishop elect of Lincoln, and afterwards Archbishop of York, a natural son of King Henry by the fair Rosamond, putting himself at the head of a body of troops, arrested the progress of the invaders. Henry now found it high time to return to England ; and immediately after his arrival hastened to the shrine of St. Thomas à Becket, already become the favourite saint of England. Here he performed a most severe penance ; and having received absolution for the supposed murder of Becket, he proceeded to London. On the very day on which his peace had been thus made with the martyred saint, namely, the twelfth of July, the Scottish king, resting in security at Alnwick, and amusing himself

with his companions at a tilting match, was suddenly
surprised by a body of English knights, and after a vigorous
resistance, was thrown from his horse and made prisoner.
The news of this capture filled Henry, and all the loyal part
of the nation, with joy, as it entirely broke up the hostile
confederacy against him.

On the tenth of August of the following year, being
St. Laurence's day,—which is indicated by the figure of the
saint just above him,—King William did homage for his
crown to the English monarch, and the Scottish prelates at
the same time acknowledged the supremacy of the English
Church. The latter event must have been very acceptable
to the whole of the English clergy, but especially to the
monks of Royston, who were under the patronage of the
saint to whose miraculous assistance this extraordinary
success was ascribed.

We may remark, that these groups have been differently
construed by Stukeley and Parkin. The latter, against all
probability, maintains that the frightened monarch
represents the Emperor Decius, in whose reign he places the
martyrdom of St. Laurence ; concluding as strangely, that
the military bishop represents Pope Sextus, a contemporary
saint. Stukeley, on the other hand, concludes that Louis
VII. of France is the monarch intended ; and supposes that
this figure commemorates his precipitate retreat on St.
Laurence's day, from the siege of Verneuil. The recent ·
discovery of the initials on the breast of the figure, seems,
however, to settle this question.

XIII.—RICHARD CŒUR DE LION AND QUEEN BERENGARIA.

Returning to the group, beneath the figure of St.
Katharine and the High Altar, we perceive two royal
personages represented on a smaller scale than the effigies

above them.   As they trench upon the tablet of the High
Altar, we may conclude that they are of a somewhat later
date.   The king stands clad in complete armour, wearing
his crown, and resting his right hand on a large kite-shaped
shield, marked with a fanciful device.   The queen, who is
only of three-quarters' length, appears on the other side of
the shield.   A crown is placed above her head, but scarcely
seems to touch it, and a veil descends from her head-dress,
on either side, down to her shoulders.   She wears an elegant
stomacher, adorned with a collar and a brooch ; and her
whole costume resembles the style and fashion of royal
ladies of the twelfth century.   Ranging on the same side
with the king, is the small crucifix already alluded to,
exhibiting the same scene as the altar above ; and beneath
it is the holy sepulchre, represented by a Norman arch, in
the interior of which is carved, in single line, a small heart,
and a large heart in double lines, (a heart of hearts,)
emblematic of intense devotion ; while beneath them is a
hand engraved with a heart, indicative of dedication to some
special service.

We can scarcely doubt, that these figures and symbols
import a vow to take the cross.

They may either represent King Henry II., who took
the vow, though he never went to the crusade ; in which
case the lady will be Queen Eleanor ; whose disgrace and
imprisonment, however, make this supposition less likely.
Or, far more probably, King Richard I., Cœur de Lion, the
most distinguished crusader of his age, and Queen
Berengaria, whom he married, and caused to be crowned on
his way to the Holy Land.   But this lady was never
crowned in England, and after her husband's death, her
rights as queen dowager were for some time denied by her
brother-in-law, King John ; a circumstance which may

possibly account for the peculiar position of the crown above noticed. This group being placed immediately below the effigy of St. Katharine and the high altar, may be likewise intended to commemorate the date of the agreement made between King Richard and Philip of France, which was in *November, 1189,* and contained a condition to unite their forces for the crusade on the following *Easter-day.*

XIV.—GENEALOGICAL FIGURES.

We now come to the long line of smaller figures, male and female, which extends below the principal groups, from the small crucifix to the effigy of St. Christopher. The personal identification of this series is altogether out of the question; but we may reasonably conclude, with Stukeley, that it represents for the most part, the principal patrons, visitors, and benefactors of the oratory, whose obits were not improbably celebrated in this place. And as many of these must certainly have been members of the noble houses, successively lords of the manor of Newsells, and other personages specially mentioned in early deeds and charters, as benefactors to the Priory, we may naturally conclude, that among them may be found representatives of the Magnaville, Rochester, Scales, Clare, Bassingbourne, Argentein, and other illustrious families of the age and neighbourhood.

This series consists of some fourteen or fifteen personages, more or less distinctly preserved.

The first figure, of which only the upper part is seen, is in close contact with the disputed shield marked with the initials H K, and if we might venture to suppose it an addition of a later period, we should infer from the historical fact of King Henry V. having specially confirmed the deeds and charters of the Royston Priory, that the good monks of the fifteenth century have here evinced their gratitude, by placing the gallant monarch and his Queen Katharine on the list of their chief benefactors, and under the special protection of the patron saint of the oratory.

The next figure is a half-length. It seems of an older type, and wears the helmet of a crusader. A youthful figure, nearly effaced, rests upon his shoulder. It is not impossible that this person may represent Geoffrey de Magnaville, the husband of Lady Rosia.

Then follow three male figures, the second wearing a round casque, or cap, and marked with a cross on his breast; then two females, in square head-dresses, the first of whom may be Lady Rosia herself; then, again, three males, the two first having hearts engraved on their breasts; the last having a cross, and a hand engraved with a heart over the right shoulder; the first and the last also wearing the helmet of a Crusader. The peculiar attributes of the last figure make it probable that William de Magnaville, the favourite son of Lady Rosia, is here intended.

Next come two females again, in square head-dresses, one of whom is marked on the bosom with a cross; and these are followed by several figures which are no longer intelligible.

The whole series appears in irregular line. The perfect figures stand erect, with arms a-kimbo, perhaps to denote that they were living personages; and the crosses and hearts, which many of them wear in common with most of the saints and martyrs in the Cave, probably indicate that those who are so represented, had either taken the vow, or were devoted to a religious life.

The following names, extracted from the earliest charters of the Priory, may enable the reader to make his own selection of the worthies for whom these portraits were possibly intended, though it is not denied, that there may be some later interpolations among them :

1. Eustace de Merks, founder of the original chapel or canonry, and lord of the manor of Newsells.
2. Ralph de Rochester, principal founder of the Priory, and also lord of the manor of Newsells.
3. Hawysia, his wife.
4. William de Rochester, his heir.
5. Alicia de Scales, daughter of Ralph, and afterwards lady of the manor.
6. Richard de Clare, Count of Gloucester, afterwards lord of the manor.
7. Waren de Bassingbourne,
8. Reginald de Argentein,
9. Margaret, Countess,
10. Juliana, } Benefactors.
11. Ralph de Reed,
12. Robert de Burn,

And last, not least, as being members of the first noble family, lords *in capite* of the manor of Newsells,

13. Geoffrey de Magnaville, husband of Lady Rosia.
14. Lady Rosia herself.
15. William de Magnaville, the distinguished crusader, and possibly founder of the oratory.

XV.—THE PEDIGREE.

It remains only to allude to certain figures between the effigy of the military bishop, and that of King William of Scotland, erroneously supposed by Stukeley to be a crucifix, but which, on closer inspection, appears rather to be a genealogical succession.   Their crowded position in this spot, as well as their subject, may certainly raise a presumption of their being a subsequent addition.   The figures of this group represent a line of three descents, one below the other, a female at the top, then a male, and a full-length female at the bottom.   Whatever be their date, they certainly resemble both in form and costume, the ladies on the other side of the Cave.   On the podium or bench immediately beneath them, is engraved a sepulchral slab of two sides, on one of which is the figure of a man, and on the other, that of a woman.   By the side of the genealogical stem there is also a family picture in miniature of three youths, who probably represent the children of the surviving lady.   We may conclude that the whole gives us the pedigree of this lady, and the interment of an ancestral pair, whose obits were most likely celebrated on this spot. And as marks of other figures are dimly seen on the podium just by, as well as near the altar of St. Thomas à Becket, it seems probable, that in these cases also, obits were performed in the Cave.

THE HERMITAGE.

We offer but one word more on the question of the Hermitage, which was the subject of another warm dispute between Stukeley and Parkin.   The idea of a hermitage in this place after the death of Lady Rosia, was rejected by Stukeley as altogether inconsistent with his theory of the origin and use of the Cave.   Parkin, who had no such chimeras to defend, maintained the continued existence of a hermitage on this spot, even from Saxon times ; and he supported his opinion by the express recital of a deed which conveyed the Priory property to the Chester family. Stukeley, notwithstanding, ridiculed the notion of a

hermitage in the midst of a town ; and Parkin replied to
this objection by citing several instances of hermitages so
situated. During the whole of the controversy, the matter
rested in mere conjecture. A fortunate discovery, however,
has recently confirmed the opinion of Parkin. For although
he appears to have mistaken a later grant from Edward VI.,
which notices a hermitage, for an earlier grant of Henry
VIII., in which no hermitage is mentioned ; and although
the hermitage recited in Edward's grant, being described as
in the manor of Hedley, and in the parish of Barkway,
could not have meant a hermitage at Royston, which was in
the manor of Newsells, and in Edward's reign had become
an independent parish : yet he was right in the main fact,
of a hermitage actually existing at Royston.

This fact has been ascertained from an entry in the old
churchwarden's book of the parish of Bassingbourne, which
extends as far back as the reign of Henry VII. ; and among
other most curious details, contains a record under date of
A.D. 1506, of the " *Gyft of 20d*" *recd* " *Off a Hermytt depting at*
Roiston i y^s pysh." It is true, that this entry does not
absolutely fix the residence of this hermit at the Cave. But
beside the improbability of there being two hermitages in so
small a town ; the position of the Cave being exactly across
the line which, in that reign, separated the parish of
Barkway from the parish of Bassingbourne, shows that a
hermit dying on that spot, would be correctly described as
departing within the limits of the latter parish ; and the
existence of a cell above the Cave, moreover, seems almost a
necessary consequence of its close proximity to the road,
and its having two shafts opening up to the surface. This
inference is also corroborated by an old manorial survey,
made about seventy years after the dissolution of the Priory,
which distinctly recognises the spot as belonging to the lord

of the manor, and records the building of the Mercat House, in a way to help the conclusion, that it probably occupied the site of an older building. This survey is dated A.D. 1610, and contains the following memorandum :

"Note : that in the myddest of Icknell Street aforesaid,
"and at the west end of the same street, there is a '*Fayr*
"*House* or *Crosse*' buylded up by the Lorde of the said
"manor, and the whole Township, for a Clock House,'and a
"Prison House, for the use and benefit of the whole Parish,
"on both sydes, as well for Cambridgeshire as for Hertford-
"shire syde, and *standing in both the said counties.*"
"By the syde of it is wrote,
"The *Clock Howse, Crosse, & Prison Howse* in
"Icknell Streete, for the whole Parishe."

CONTINUED USE AND FINAL ABANDONMENT OF THE ORATORY.

Our investigations thus far, have led us to the conclusion, that the dedication of the ancient Cave to the purpose of a Christian oratory, and the execution of the greater part of its sculptures, may be assigned, with greatest probability, to the period of the Crusades, and about the reigns of Henry II. and Richard Cœur de Lion. We have been obliged, notwithstanding, to dismiss Dr. Stukeley's fanciful theory in favour of Lady Rosia, as inconsistent with probability ; and on that subject we have now only to add the testimony of Leland, that she was really buried at Chickesand, in Bedfordshire, in a nunnery there, founded by herself ; and where she spent the close of her life in religious seclusion. Our concluding remarks will also furnish a satisfactory account of the skull and other human bones discovered in the loose earth which afterwards filled the Cave.

The frequency of the religious services celebrated in this oratory, must of course be open to conjecture. We may, perhaps, infer that they were limited to the great festivals of the church, and the holidays of the particular saints who figure in it ; to the obits of benefactors ; to occasional masses for distinguished pilgrims and visitors ; and to the private devotions of the resident hermit or hermits. We have as little certainty as to the religious order to which the hermit of the Cave belonged. But it seems probable that as the monks of the Priory belonged to the order of St. Augustine, the Augustine Eremites would be preferred for the service of the oratory.

That the Cave was used for religious purposes long after the time of Richard I. does not admit of reasonable doubt ; but the exact period of its abandonment is not so certain. It has been supposed by some, that this event occurred in the reign of Henry IV., when the town was almost consumed by fire. But the careful filling up of the place argues a deliberate purpose. There is little question, indeed, that the Cave was open until the period of the Reformation, when it passed, with other ecclesiastical property, into the hands of the Crown ; and on its subsequent transfer to the Chester family, being no longer required for superstitious services, and useless for any other, it underwent the common fate of the Priory and the Free Chapel of St. Nicholas, and was shortly after closed and forgotten.

That this step was taken before the age of Iconoclasm, seems highly probable, from the unmutilated condition of the principal figures. And as the age of the Reformation was one in which such desecrations were too frequent to attract particular notice, or to leave behind any vivid impressions, it will best explain the oblivion into which the

very existence of the Cave, as well as the exact sites of the
Priory, and of the Free Chapel of St. Nicholas, speedily fell.
We may conclude, that at the same time the ancient cross
itself disappeared.   This period will also account most
satisfactorily for the mode of filling up the Cave, as well as
for the discovery of human bones and mediæval pottery ;
for then it was, that the Priory and cloisters being taken
down, the site was appropriated to the new manor house
and gardens, the building and arrangement of which
necessarily required the removal of much rubbish, and the
clearing away of many bones.   Some of these we know to
have been afterwards deposited in the church ; but a portion
of them would be very naturally employed by the lord of the
manor, to fill up the oratory, preparatory to the erection of
the mercat house and prison above it.   The utter contempt
with which popery was afterwards regarded, must have
extinguished all desire on the part of the town's people to
perpetuate the memory of a former superstition ; and as
they had long ceased to be Romanists before they became
archæologists, no further interest was felt by any one in the
subject.

We offer a few concluding remarks on the Arabic
numerals recently discovered in the Cave.   And, first
respecting the date of 1347, already noticed as being in the
dome.   The care with which these figures are cut, their
general air of antiquity, and their obscure and almost
inacessible position, would certainly have placed them
beyond suspicion, but for a single figure (the figure 4), which
seems open to challenge, as differing in some degree from
the usual form of the fourteenth century.   Yet the falsifica-
tion of these figures seems most improbable.   It is next to
certain, that neither Stukeley nor Parkin was aware of their
existence ; for had they been, the former must, as a point of

honour, and the latter assuredly would, as a ground of triumph, have adverted to them. Indeed, we have it in proof, that no early antiquaries examined this part of the Cave ; and since their time, we can conceive of no motive which could prompt any one to attempt a deception.

The peculiarity in the form of this numeral must, nevertheless, be admitted. Yet it is certain, that such a form was occasionally used about the middle of the fifteenth century ; and the exact period when the circular shape of the old numeral merged into the angular, or by what gradations, if any, this was effected, is not precisely known. It is clear that the figure here has a transition character ; and contemporaneous manuscripts exist, which justify the belief, that as early as the middle of the fourteenth century, the disputed form may, in some instances, have been used.

These, however, are not the only ancient numerals that have been discovered. We have another instance, just above the prison cell of St. Katharine, apparently written by an amateur hand in old English characters, with the name of "Martin," and the date of 18 February, 1350 ; and in this case the figures themselves offer no insuperable objection to their authenticity. Supposing these inscriptions to be genuine, they furnish decisive proof of the continued use of the oratory up to that time. In regard to the numerals in the dome, they also seem to mark the date of certain alterations or repairs to the eastern shaft, which we must conceive to have been then the principal entrance ; and judging from the colouring on the block itself, we may further imagine that they indicate the period of the painting of the figures, a practice which, from other sources, we know to have been much in vogue in the reign of Edward III.

If, on the other hand, we are obliged to conclude that a fraud has been practised, it would most probably consist in the change of a figure 5 into the figure 3, which would then give us the year 1547—a year remarkable for the first act of parliament which suppressed idolatry and superstition throughout the land. But in this case we must also infer from the insertion of the date, that it was done with the hope that at some further time the oratory might be again opened and used.

However the case be decided, it will be clear that the final exit from the Cave was made through the northern shaft, which afterwards led to its discovery.

RECAPITULATION.

The result of our whole inquiry will appear in the following conclusions :—

1. That the Cave was first formed by means of shafts, either of British or Romano-British construction, and at a period anterior to Christianity.

2.   That at a somewhat later period, the Cave was used as a Roman sepulchre.

3.   That about the period of the Crusades, it received the greater part of its present decorations, and was then, if not before, converted into a Christian oratory, to which a hermitage was probably attached.

4.   That it remained open until the Reformation, whe it was finally filled up, closed, and forgotten.

DESCRIPTION OF PLATES.

PLATE 1.

No.
1. The High Altar.
2. St. Christopher.
3. Legend of St. Katharine.
4. Effigy of St. Katharine.
13. Richard Cœur de Lion and Queen Berengaria.
14. Genealogical Figures.

PLATE 2.

5. The Cross of St. Helena.
6. The Holy Family.
7. St. Laurence.
8. The Conversion of St. Paul.
9. William the Lion, King of Scots.
10. Queen Eleanor.
11. The Shrine of St. John Baptist and St. Thomas à Becket.
12. King Henry II.
15. The Pedigree.

PLATE 3.

1. Section of the Cave, looking west; with the two Shafts.
2. Appearance of the Cave when half opened.
3. Ground Plan of the Cave, and the Grave.
4. Anglo-Norman Architecture.
5. Norman Arch.
6. The Disputed Shield.
7. Kite-shaped Shield.
8. Crown of Richard Cœur de Lion.
9. Crown of Queen Berengaria.
10. Crown of St. Katharine.
11. Circular Shield.
12. Another Shield.
13. Crown of William King of Scots.
14. The Date in the Dome.
15. Lady's Head-dress.
16. The Seal found in the Cave.
17. The Sword of St. Paul.
18. Low-crowned Helmet of Henry II.
19. Another Shield.
20. Crusader's Helmet.
21. Head-dress of the Virgin at the Cross.
22. Second Date in the Cave.
23. Crown of Queen Eleanor.
24. Hearts in Double and Triple Lines.
25. Initials of William King of Scots.

INDEX.

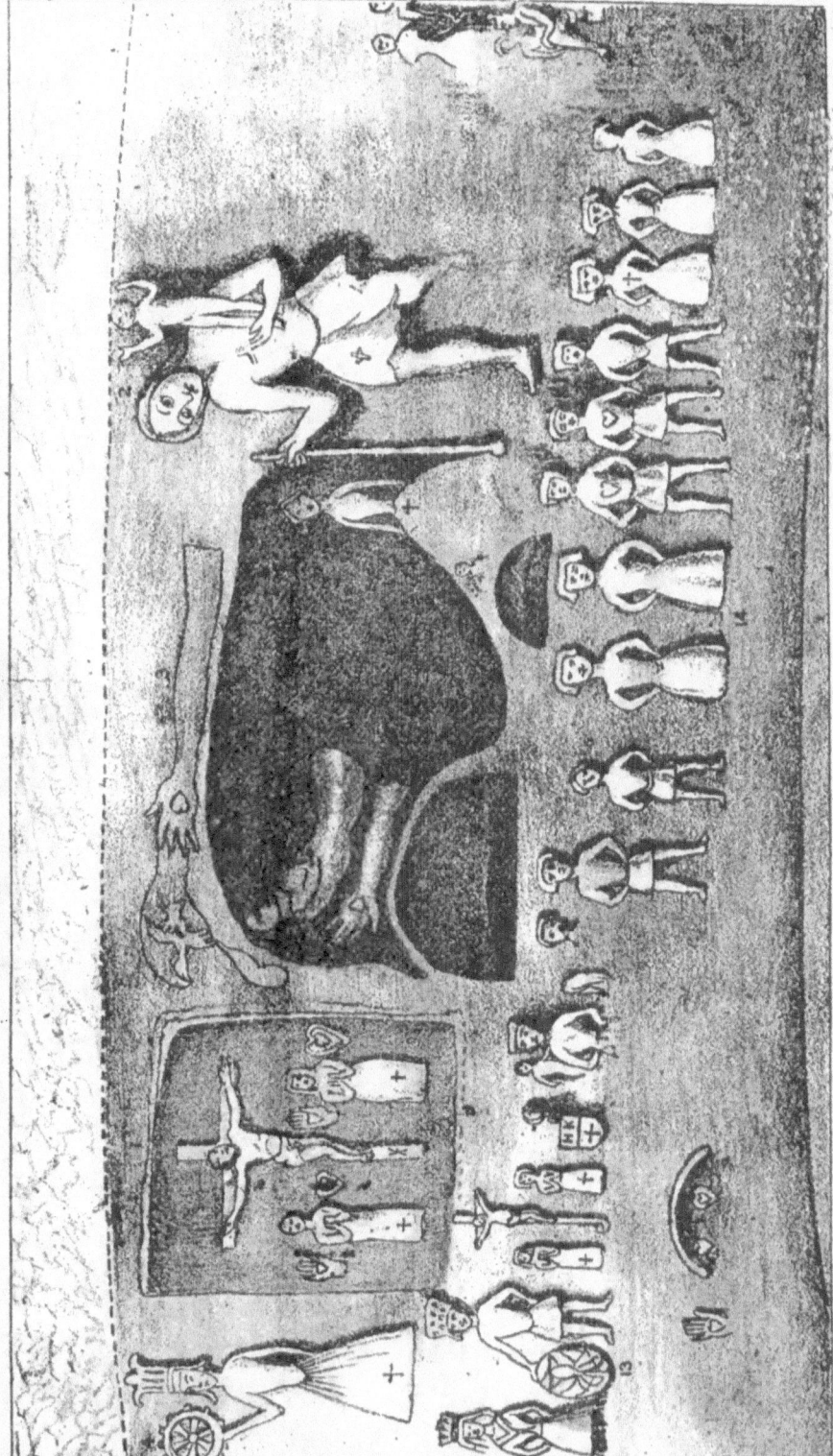

PLATE I. SECTION OF CAVE LOOKING NORTHWARDS.

Drawn by Mr J. Beldam.

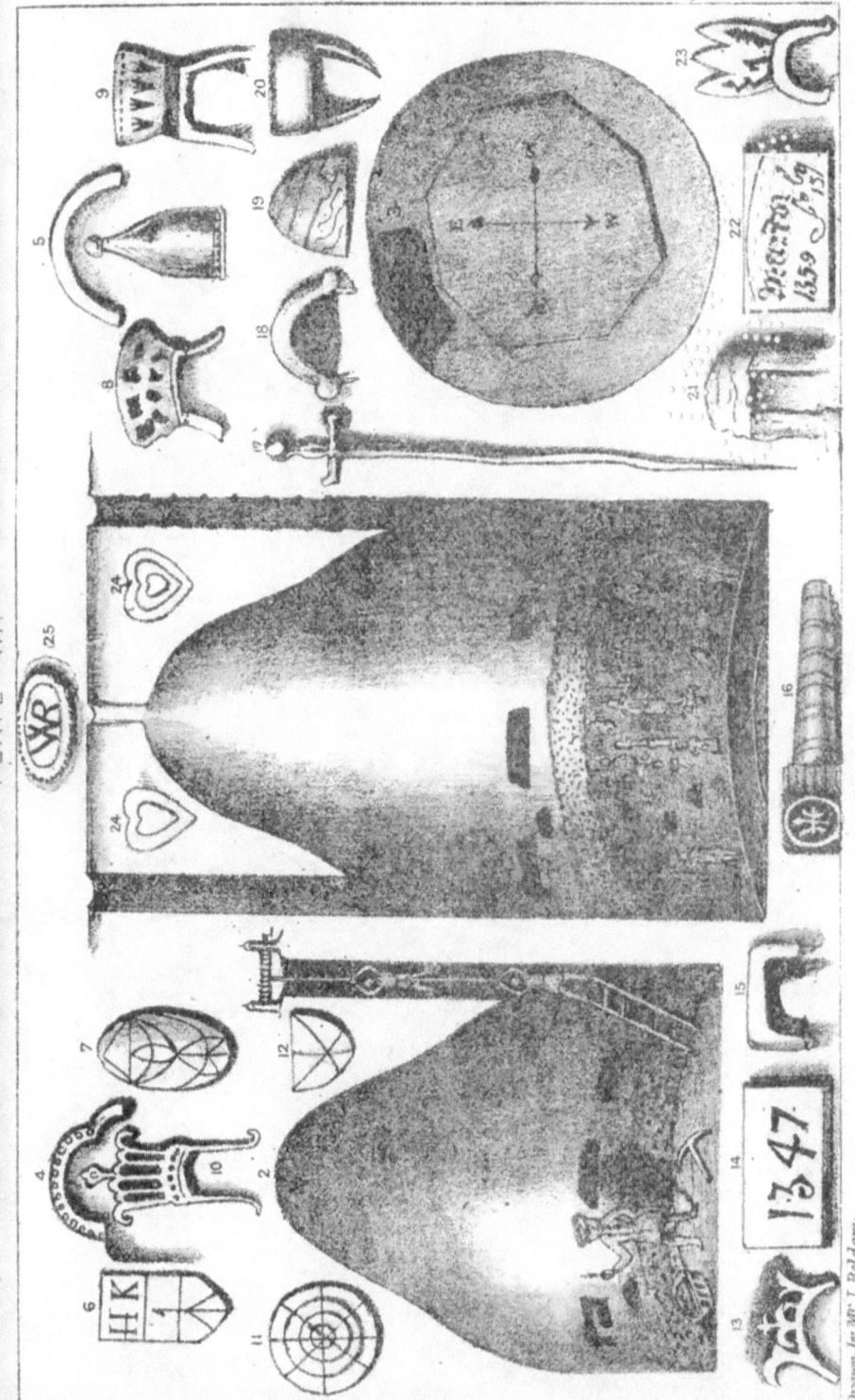

Drawn by Mr J Beldam.